DUNGEONS & DRAGONS®

A Goblin Problem!

BY
DIANE WALKER

ILLUSTRATED BY
TIM PROBERT

HARPER**Chapters**

An Imprint of HarperCollinsPublishers

Library of Congress Control Number: 2021953154
ISBN 978-0-06-303918-6

22 23 24 25 26   WOR   10 9 8 7 6 5 4 3 2 1

First Edition

TABLE OF CONTENTS

All About Monsters

Every day before school, Zellidora "Zelli" Stormclash thinks about three things. First, did the homework get done? Answer: Yes. Well, *usually*. Second, are your horns and tail in place? Answer: Definitely. Always. And third, which monster will be a problem? Answer: Probably all of them.

Zelli quietly walks down the hall of the legendary Dungeon Academy. She passes goblins, slimes, and all sorts of creatures. Zelli goes right to her locker. Her locker is a big treasure chest. To open the chest, Zelli must undo a clever trap! The magical lock must be tapped five times in a special rhythm. Then the chest will open safely. Inside are books and other things students need at monster school. The treasure chest holds pencils, a wooden practice sword, a pouch for trinkets, and a snack. It also has a small mirror. Zelli looks at herself in the mirror and checks her

disguise. She notices her horns are on straight and smiles. Zelli is the only human at Dungeon Academy. Humans are not liked very much at this school! To fit in Zelli must pretend to be a monster. This was a lot of work for her.

Zelli's locker also holds special things like trophies and trinkets. Monster students have given her these for helping them with bullies. The monsters gave her things like magic rocks, bowls of gunk, rings, and necklaces made of teeth. Zelli has become a kind of protector at the school. The monsters who aren't so good at being scary, mean, spooky, or slimy sometimes need her help. At Dungeon Academy, it's important to be the absolute scariest you can be.

After all, the monsters there are training for a life in the dungeons. They will grow up to watch over gold and keep human adventurers away!

Zelli gathers her school books. "I wonder if anyone will need my help today," she says to herself. "I hope not. Helping with bullies all the time tires me out."

But it will not be a boring day. Behind her, a little kobold boy wanders by. He is mumbling about a lost pendant. He will have to go to the lost and found by the main office.

Maybe I should help him, thinks Zelli. But when she turns around, he is already lost in the crowd of monsters and creatures who are off to their next class. Zelli's first class after lunch is History of Horrible Humans. Monster children go to learn all about the famous human adventurers! She finds her manual on horrible humans under a mess of thank-you notes and gifts from the monsters she has helped. Most recently, she helped a frog creature named Gixi.

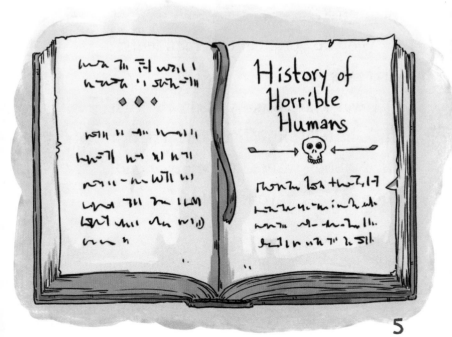

Gixi sits next to her during History of Horrible Humans. He has green skin and smells like a pond. That morning, he sees Zelli at her locker and stops to say hello. He pokes her in the elbow and says, "Thank you again for helping me in the library!"

With a huff, Zelli looks away. She doesn't want all this attention, not when she is in disguise. "Don't mention it."

"Why do you help other students?" Gixi asks.

"I was scared like you on my first day," she tells him. "Everyone stared at me. Nobody wanted to be my friend. I don't think anyone should feel that way."

Gixi doesn't know that Zelli is a human. She hides it with a tail and horns, to pretend to be like the minotaurs who found and raised her. Zelli isn't so afraid anymore. She's been at the school for years, but she knows what it's like to stick out. A big bell rings, and Gixi hurries away. Classes are about to begin.

Zelli closes her locker trunk and notices a scrap of paper by her boots. She picks it up and reads it.

Dear Zelli,
My name is Bucket, and I need your help! Everyone says you are the best against bullies. Vermin is the biggest goblin bully of all! She calls me pretty and says I have perfect skin. It's so mean! Come to the Goreball field after classes if you want to help.

Bucket

"Oh well," Zelli says with a sigh. "Just another day at Dungeon Academy."

You read one chapter. That's over 707 words!

A Day at Dungeon Academy

Zelli goes to History of Horrible Humans with a bad feeling in her stomach. It's not just because she skipped lunch. Now she knows that she will have to help Bucket, and it makes her nervous.

I shouldn't help so many monster kids, Zelli thinks as she leaves behind her locker trunk. She begins the walk to the lower dungeons. *It's going to bring attention I don't want.*

I'm trying to blend in! I will be in a lot of trouble if the monsters find out I am a human.

And she is trying to blend in. A girl like Zelli can't help it. Her minotaur mothers, Iasme and Kifin, raised her to be brave and strong.

"Being brave and strong," Zelli mumbles to herself, "means never letting someone small get stepped on."

You might think with all this talk of Zelli being strong that she is covered in muscles like her minotaur mothers. But she isn't!

She is not particularly big or small. There are many larger, scarier monsters at the school. Zelli just knows what her mothers taught her. They taught that it's all right to scare other kids in Haunting 101 or when playing Goreball. But they also told her that showing off roaring all the time or being a bully is for monsters who secretly feel small inside. At first, it was hard for Zelli to understand this.

"But I'm supposed to be scary!" she would tell her parents. "I'm trying to be a monster like you!"

After all, there were a lot of rules at Dungeon Academy that made her mothers' lessons confusing. Being too nice and too quiet could get you in trouble and land you in detention (and Zelli did NOT want to go to detention!). Helping others was allowed in Pack Hunting by Night class. Being a team player was also allowed on the Goreball field. Other than

that, it was every scale-face and fuzzball for themselves!

"You will know when it's time to be tough and scary," her mother Kifin said. She was a professor at Dungeon Academy and always spoke like a teacher. "But you will also know when it's better to be kind. When you've done wrong, it will feel like you swallowed a really squirmy worm."

"Ew!" young Zelli had cried back.

But now Zelli understands that worm feeling. It happened the first time she saw an older owlbear push a kobold down and laugh. An owlbear is just that: the body of a big bear with the head of an owl. But kobolds are much smaller and look like short lizards who can walk on two feet. Zelli didn't help, and suddenly the worm feeling came. She liked it better to not have worms wriggling in her stomach.

Not So Tall

Not So Mean

VERY TALL

KIND OF MEAN

17

So Zelli kept to herself to make sure the other students wouldn't find out she was a human. Like the humans they learned about in their History of Horrible Humans class.

"Class!" she says to herself. "I'm going to be late!" Zelli quickly follows goblins, owlbears, slaadi, and kobolds. They all hurry toward a spiral staircase that goes down into the lower dungeons.

"Wait for me!" a voice calls from behind her.

TROPHIES

19

The voice surprises her, and Zelli spins around too fast, losing her balance and almost tumbling into the bottomless pit next to the spiral stairs.

A huge, furry hand reaches for her. "Watch out!"

You read two chapters. That's over 1,278 words!

3

Hugo,
the Vegan Owlbear

"I'm going to fall!" cries Zelli, holding on to the fuzzy paw for dear life.

"Up you go!"

Suddenly, Zelli is hoisted through the air and lands softly on her feet. She backs away from the edge and shakes her head.

"Thanks for the assist," she tells Hugo.

Hugo smiles. "My pleasure." Hugo is an owlbear. He has a shiny curved beak and claws.

Hugo doesn't like using his beak or claws for anything but picking flowers, snipping plants, and eating salads. Unlike his fellow owlbears, Hugo does not eat meat. He also does not like being scary. Hugo's favorite class is From Stinkweed to Witch Grass: Recognizing the Flora of the Forgotten Realms.

In many ways, he's like Zelli. They are both different and strange, but in a good way.

"We should hurry," Hugo tells her. He carries a leather bag on his hip that is always overflowing with herbs and plants. "Professor Gast gets so angry when we're late!"

Hugo is right, and so they rush down the slippery, cracked steps. Dungeon Academy is quite dangerous. The entire school is made of stone and wood. There are creepy corners, cobwebbed halls, and staircases that lead to nowhere.

"Did you do the reading?" Hugo asks. He is always a good and hard-working student. He is also the president of the Lurking Club. In Lurking Club, students practice hiding in the shadows and being sneaky. Hugo loves to lurk, but also to read and learn. He especially likes to learn about nature.

"Yes, last night I read all about the terrible triumphs of Rotver the Rakish. He stole a whole cave's worth of gold from goblins."

Hugo shivers, feathers and fur flying everywhere. The air gets cold as they reach the bottom of the stairs and enter the lower dungeons. "I am ever so glad I will never meet him. What a horrible human!"

Zelli nods, distracted.

"Oh. Forgive me!" Hugo lowers his voice and whispers. "Not all humans are horrible. But he was."

24

Hugo knows Zelli's secret, and he would never tell on her. That's because they are close friends who have gone on many adventures together. This was a surprise to Zelli, who did not think she would make monster friends at all.

"Are you well?" Hugo asks as they stand outside the tall, crooked doors of Professor Gast's classroom. "Is your mind somewhere else?"

"A goblin girl wants my help," says Zelli, chewing her lip. "It sounds like trouble for her, but I'm getting a reputation. I don't want to draw too much attention to myself."

Hugo glances at her fake horns and nods. "But it is who you are, Zelli. You help others."

"Maybe I help too much."

The other students head into class, and the big pendulum above is about to ring again. "I could join you," Hugo suggests. "You do not have to face bullies alone."

"No, no!" Zelli shakes her head and goes into the classroom. It's a drippy, dreary place. Professor Gast, who is a floating, flaming head, glares at them. They are almost late, and that is enough to make him angry.

"I can do this alone. I don't want you to get hurt."

"But—"

Hugo cannot finish his thought. At the front of class, Professor Gast clears his throat as the big pendulum clangs throughout the halls. Class begins, and Zelli scurries to her seat. She is hoping the professor does not call on her for answers. Her mind is somewhere else, thinking about a poor goblin girl called Bucket.

Maybe I shouldn't help so much, Zelli thinks to herself, opening her textbook to page forty-five.

You read three chapters. That's over 1,889 words!

4

Bauble
(The Know-it-All)

Zelli is so lost her in own thoughts that she does not realize she has taken a seat next to Bauble.

Bauble is a mimic. A mimic is an amazing creature that can take on almost any form. It can turn into a treasure chest, a carriage, or a sword. It can also be all other sorts of things to trick anyone and everyone. Mimics are full of surprises. Bauble likes to take the form of a thick, dusty, fussy book. Like a book, Bauble is full of knowledge. The cover of this living book has eyes and teeth. It's not exactly like other books you might own. When Professor Gast isn't looking, Bauble flutters their pages and sends a scrap of paper from their desk to Zelli's.

Professor Gast is lecturing about Rotver the Rakish when the scrap lands on Zelli's desk. Zelli glances in every direction, then hides the message in her hand and reads.

To you,
Study buddy session after school? I'll bring the slime punch
from Us

Zelli groans. Bauble always, ALWAYS wants to study. She will never understand how one small mimic can hold so much information.

Can't, Zelli scribbles with her pencil. To her right, Hugo is watching all of this. He is always curious. Zelli thinks about telling Bauble what she's up to, but she doesn't want to get anyone else in trouble. It's dangerous to help other students too much. It could land them all in detention in the lava cave, which none of them want. (The rumor is that a dozen students have perished there of sheer boredom. Gulp!)

She doesn't write anything else, and when Professor Gast floats away to read off the chalkboard, Zelli flicks the scrap back to Bauble.

Bauble frowns, looking very disappointed indeed. Zelli doesn't like keeping things from her friends. It feels wrong to ignore Bucket and let the bullies win.

After an hour of Professor Gast's droning, the bell clangs again. Zelli claps her book closed and dashes out of her seat. She dodges around a bugbear and a yawning ooze. She is trying to outrun both Bauble and Hugo. They do not have class with her next (Advanced Roaring), so she might be able to avoid their questions. They don't need to get involved with helping Bucket. After all, they could get hurt! Zelli has tangled with bullies before, and she knows what it takes. Bauble and Hugo are not like her—they stay out of such trouble.

Zelli heaves a sigh of relief as she reaches the stairs out of the dungeon much faster than

Hugo and Bauble. But as she starts the quick climb upward, she feels a sharp tug on her tunic.

"Not sssooo fassst!"

You read four chapters. That's over 2,347 words!

The Not-So-Average Kobold

"Let go!" Zelli says, laughing at the little kobold.

"Sssnabla wants to know why you run!" her short little friend says. Snabla always carries his shield. It's a crummy old thing that hangs off his narrow shoulders. It's a special magic shield, but that's a secret. Only Snabla and his friends know that his shield is wearing a disguise, like Zelli. Snabla's scaly ears stick straight up, and he speaks with a lisp, his forked tongue poking out.

A kobold is like a dog-lizard creature, small and wily. Kobolds are pointy, with claws, a tail, jagged teeth, and a narrow snout. Snabla is not much taller than Zelli's knobby knees. His favorite subject is anything about dragons. Snabla tells everyone he is related to dragons.

"You never run to classs! Not like sssilly know-it-all sssuck-up Bauble. Ssso why does Zelli run?"

Snabla is right. Only Bauble and Hugo are obsessed enough with learning to rush between classes.

"I . . ." Zelli doesn't like to lie. "I . . . forgot something in my trunk. I have to run up and get it before roaring class."

"Sssnabla have ssstinky Dwarven Delvesss with Professor Bonebrain. Not far from your trunk! Sssnabla come with!"

"Oh." Zelli sighs. She doesn't really have to go to her locker trunk. Now Snabla will know she's not telling him the whole truth. "Listen, I don't actually need to go that way. I just want to be alone right now."

"Why alone? Danger Club no go alone! Bauble and Hugo not far behind. We wait for them!"

Zelli continues quickly up the stairs, the air getting warmer as she goes. Snabla huffs and

puffs to keep up on his much stubbier legs. "Not this time, Snabla. Thanks, but . . . I just have something I need to do alone. I'll explain later!"

Can she? She begins to wonder why she wants

to help Bucket alone. There's strength  in numbers, and her friends are brave, too.

One day all this standing up for other students will land me in real trouble, Zelli realizes. *Everyone will find out I'm not really a minotaur. Then Snabla, Hugo, and Bauble will be in trouble for keeping my secret.*

No, she has to keep them out of it.

But still, she will go to the Goreball field and help Bucket. It's the right thing to do and something her mothers taught her to do. Yet sometimes the right thing to do is not easy. Sometimes, the right thing to do is very . . . scary.

① ② ③ ④ ⑤ ⑥ ⑦ ⑧ ⑨ ⑩

How to Save
a Goblin

Zelli isn't an expert on everything monster related like Bauble, so she takes her free period and goes to the library. From Bauble, Zelli learned that sometimes research is the best defense. It can also be the best offense. The library isn't like any ordinary library, but then, what *is* ordinary at Dungeon Academy? Six levels tall, the library is a damp cavern filled

to the brim. It has scrolls, books, parchments, tablets, and tomes. It's a zigzagging wonderland of pages, dust, and secrets! Zelli hid there a lot before she became part of the Danger Club, so she knows the place well.

Finding the Behavior section, Zelli looks for anything useful about goblins. Zelli thinks that if she can understand their strengths and weaknesses, she can outsmart Vermin and keep her from bullying Bucket again. As Zelli finds a stack of books to take into a hidden corner, she wonders what the elf and dwarven manuals might say about goblins. They might say they are small and creepy. They might also say they like to live in caves and mines, they're smelly and mean, but they're also strangely great dancers? The goblins Zelli knows would probably take that as a list of compliments.

Curling up in her nook, Zelli cracks open an old, creaky volume entitled *Goblins: Rat Keepers and Wolf Riders*. It is filled with soaring pictures of goblins riding into battle on shaggy animals, clubs raised over their heads. Zelli frowns and closes her eyes—

the first ever student who called her names was a goblin. She had only just started at the academy, and she was frightened of everything. She was afraid of the smell, the cold, twisty hallways, and the traps littering the corridors. She mostly remembers the unfamiliar creatures who looked at her oddly. Her mothers, Iasme and Kifin, had tried their best to get her ready. Professor Kifin Stormclash even taught physical education, but having her nearby didn't make all the fear go away. And Zelli wasn't about to run to her mother and tattle whenever she had a hard day. After all, minotaurs were supposed to be tough and totally unruffled.

But an older goblin boy named Mudmaw cornered her in the dining hall. She was already sitting alone. He came over anyway to bother and poke fun at her. All his friends were there to watch as he knocked over her mug of milk and tried to pull on her horn.

"What kind of minotaur are you, anyway?" he asked, laughing. "You're so small and weak, even a kobold could best you!"

Zelli had been so overwhelmed, she didn't

know what to do. She let them point and sneer. After they left, she sat there shivering, her tunic soaked in milk. A hundred clever things came to mind, but it was too late.

"I won't let that happen again," she told herself that day. "Minotaurs are tough as nails, so that's what I'll be."

"And clever, too," Zelli says to the goblin book on her lap. The memory fades, and she begins to study. She can picture Bucket at that

same lunch table, cowering as Vermin calls her names. *Brave and clever*, Zelli thinks, *that's what I'll be. Not just for Bucket, but for First Day of School Zelli, who just hadn't earned her horns yet.*

She reads quickly, wanting to make the most of her free hour. Suddenly she finds the right passage!

Goblins are ruled by the strongest or smartest among them . . .

Goblins are ruled by the strongest or smartest among them...

The strongest *or* smartest. That is the key!

"If I can convince Vermin that Bucket is pretty but also smart, maybe Vermin will start to see Bucket as an equal," Zelli whispers.

She closes the book and smiles. "Bauble would be proud."

You read six chapters. That's over 3,408 words!

Zelli to the Rescue

All through her next class (Climbing and Ropemaking), Zelli can only think about how she will stop Vermin. She doesn't know the goblin personally, but Vermin has a reputation. Everyone at Dungeon Academy knows that Vermin is the strongest, ugliest, most scarred goblin in their grade. She

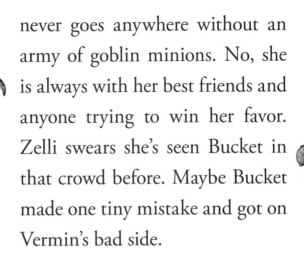

never goes anywhere without an army of goblin minions. No, she is always with her best friends and anyone trying to win her favor. Zelli swears she's seen Bucket in that crowd before. Maybe Bucket made one tiny mistake and got on Vermin's bad side.

The strongest *or* the smartest. Zelli thinks about it over and over while Professor Thork, a very strong kobold, shows six different ways to tie off a climbing rope. She scribbles notes and waits for the pendulum to clang. When it does, she scoops up her things and hurries down the main hall toward wide doors that lead out onto the Goreball fields. This is where her mother usually teaches, but today there are only a

handful of bugbears. They are in the distance, tossing a disk back and forth. The sky is iron gray and dark, a hard wind blowing down the sides of the mountain that conceals the school. A few raindrops splatter on Zelli's nose as she searches for Bucket.

Finally, she spots the little goblin near a dirty shed where the Goreball equipment is kept.

She's just as Zelli remembers—short, slender, with smooth yellowish-green skin and orange eyes. Wearing a white dress, she couldn't look more different from Vermin, who goes everywhere draped in leather, fur, and claws.

Zelli runs over to Bucket. "You wanted to meet?"

The goblin pushes away from the shed and smiles. "You came!"

Even her voice is pretty, which the other

goblins must hate.

"I got your note," Zelli tells her. "Something about Vermin bothering you?"

"So it's true," Bucket replies. Her eyes get bigger and glossier, and suddenly Zelli has that squirming worm in her stomach. "The other students whisper that you help out, that you take on bullies. It's really true! You're the Bully Crusher!"

"Shh." Zelli presses her finger to her lips.

"Keep it down. That's a secret."

Suddenly Bucket grins. "Not anymore." She whistles loudly. The shed door slams open. Six goblins, led by Vermin, march out to surround the human. Zelli reaches for the practice wooden sword on her back, but Vermin quickly jumps forward and smacks it away.

Bucket laughs and laughs. "Ha! You're so gullible! You fell right into our trap!"

"But I came to help you," Zelli whispers. "What is this?"

"I can't believe the professors haven't put you in detention for helping so much," Bucket says, shaking her head.

The other goblins are just as disgusted with Zelli. They growl and show her their teeth. "You think you're so special," Bucket continues. "Just because you're the only minotaur at school doesn't mean you can do whatever you want! It's time for payback!"

Zelli doesn't like going to her mother for help. In that moment, she glances around the field looking for Professor Stormclash. But Zelli's alone, surrounded, and outnumbered.

The strongest *or* the smartest.

"It's just a rumor," Zelli tells them. "I can't help what other kids say about me."

"You can't talk your way out of this," Vermin sneers. "You're not the bully crusher you think you are."

In that moment, Zelli realizes her mother isn't coming.

1 2 3 4 5 6 7

8

The Legend of the Horned Razorbeast

"Why are you so small?" Vermin asks, poking Zelli's horns. One of the other goblins kicks Zelli's sword away and into the tall grass. Vermin slowly circles Zelli, belittling her with every step. "You have to be the tiniest minotaur in the whole world! Where are your muscles? Where is your fur? Aren't minotaurs supposed to have a nose ring? Too shrimpy to earn that, are you? You probably won't get your own labyrinth!"

"Not if she stays that weak and puny," Bucket adds with a sniff.

"Be quiet, Bucket. Your part in this is over!" Vermin shouts back.

Bucket ducks her head. She shuffles a few steps behind Vermin and looks sad.

"I'm not afraid of you," says Zelli. She must think of a way out of this. Usually, she's only up against one bully, not an entire group of them! Zelli looks around. The bugbears playing with the disk are too far to hear her scream for help. Zelli gulps hard. *This may be it*, she thinks.

"What's that?" cries one of the goblins to her left.

Zelli notices it, too—a towering shadow

falling across them all. It's coming from around the equipment shed, a shadow large enough to swallow the entire group. Taller than any of them, it's wide and horned. The shadow has a pointed head and what appears to be a massive sword in hand. The goblins and Zelli freeze, their eyes wide with fear. Suddenly the shadow begins to growl. Then it gives a low, snarling howl that Zelli recognizes.

"Run, you fools!" she screams. "Save yourselves! Don't you . . . Don't you know what that is?"

"No!" Vermin stamps her foot, but she's starting to shake. "What . . . What is that thing?"

"Why, it's . . . it's the Legendary Horned Razorbeast. It's loose! Loosed from the deepest pits of the Dungeon Academy dungeons!" Zelli tosses her hands in front of her face, pretending to shiver and cower. "The bloodthirsty, ten-

foot-tall terror that preys on bullies. It really hates goblin bullies, and roams the halls and fields when class lets out! It's come! You summoned it!"

You read eight chapters. That's over 4,344 words!

Danger Club
to the Rescue!

"V-Vermin?" Bucket stammers. "That thing is awfully big . . ."

"Too big!" the goblin to her left shrieks. "I'm out of here!"

"You can't leave me!" Vermin shouts back. "Us! I mean, you can't leave us! You coward!"

But the whole goblin pack begins to retreat from the shed. They try to hide behind Zelli.

"I've never heard of this thing," Vermin insists.

But even she begins to shy away from the equipment shed.

"You should pay more attention in class," Zelli tells her. "The Horned Razorbeast hates bullies. That's why it's here! If you keep bothering students and making them feel small, it will come back! Why do you think the other bullies leave me alone? They know I'm protected by the legendary beast! You would know it, too, if you spent more time doing homework and less time being awful!"

That one, Zelli thinks, was for Bauble. She can just imagine the little mimic cheering.

"We w-won't bother anyone else!" Bucket promises, glued to Vermin's side. But Vermin pushes her away and scoffs.

"Speak for yourself!" Vermin cries with fear. She folds her arms across her leather vest.

At that moment, the Legendary Horned Razorbeast lets loose a ferocious howl. The sound scatters the goblins! They all run back toward the school and away from the shed.

"W-Wait for me!" Vermin yells as she runs away. She gives one last terrified glance over her shoulder as she goes. "Fine! I w-won't bully anymore! I promise! Just don't eat me! Don't eat me!"

When the last goblin disappears, the Legendary Horned Razorbeast makes its presence known. Just as Zelli suspected,

it's composed of her friends! Hugo makes up most of the shadow. Snabla is perched on his shoulders to make the pointed head and horns. Bauble is in Hugo's hand, transformed into nothing more than a gardening rake. They all tumble to the ground and shake with laughter.

"Not sssooo brave now, are you?" Snabla kicks his feet into the ground. He is holding his belly from the force of his amusement. "Did you sssee them run?"

"Good thinking with the Razorbeast, Zelli," Bauble adds, transforming back into a book.

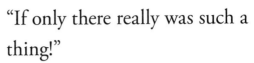

"If only there really was such a thing!"

"But there is, in a way," Hugo points out. He is the first to climb to his feet, feathers lightly ruffled as he grins at Zelli. "Now Vermin and Bucket will tell the tale of the ferocious Razorbeast, and that makes it true. Just a legend, but it will keep other students safe from bullies."

"Thanks for rescuing me," Zelli tells them, glancing up at the sky as it begins to rain in earnest. "We should get somewhere dry."

"My pages are getting wet!" Bauble cries, distressed.

Hugo picks them up and puts Bauble in his pack, leading the others back toward the warmer, drier (but not that warm or dry) halls of the academy.

"How did you know where to find me?" Zelli asks as they go.

Snabla is still chortling.

"We're the Danger Club, remember?" Bauble says cheerfully. "Where you go, we go."

You read nine chapters. That's over 4,864 words!

① ② ③ ④ ⑤ ⑥ ⑦ ⑧ ⑨ ⑩

Study Buddies

In the end, Bauble got their way. They often did. The friends wound up in the mimic's dorm room. It's a cozy, cramped space covered from floor to ceiling in aged scrolls of Bauble's favorite monster philosophers, writers, poets, and legends.

Zelli thinks the Horned Razorbeast might belong on those walls now, too.

True to their word, Bauble has brought out slime punch for everyone. Hugo chooses instead to munch on a bundle of fragrant herbs. Hugo sits with his back pushed against Bauble's little bed. Outside, a storm begins. Rain is falling hard on the mountain as distant thunder rumbles above. It makes Zelli glad for the safety of Bauble's dorm room.

While Bauble decides which quiz they will study for, Zelli gazes around at her unlikely collection of friends.

"I shouldn't have tried to do that alone," she tells them. "I needed your help. I was worried I would get you all in trouble.

My secret—"

"Is safe with all of us," Hugo says. "We keep telling you, we're your friends!"

"I know that," says Zelli. Her heart feels heavy. At least the worm feeling is no longer in her stomach. "I was just trying to protect you."

"Friendsss protect each other, sssilly!" cries Snabla, plunging his snout into his cup of punch. The punch turns his snout a funny green color.

"I never like to admit that Snabla is right," says Bauble, perched on their bed. "But Snabla is right. This time. You're not alone, Zelli. We're the Legendary Horned Razorbeast! We're the Danger Club! We're the best of friends, and we're all going to get through Dungeon Academy together."

Zelli nods and grins. This might be the day she tries Bauble's famous slime punch. "You know," says Zelli, "monsters leave me all kinds of gifts for helping them. My trunk is full of them. Tomorrow, you should all come and pick one out. You've earned it."

"Yesss!" shouts Snabla. "Presentsss!"

Zelli tries the punch, and just as she expected, it's truly disgusting. Luckily, Snabla is right there beside her and eager to finish her cup.

The strongest *or* the smartest. Luckily, Zelli's friends are both.

You read ten chapters. That's over 5,226 words!

CONGRATULATIONS!

You've read **10** chapters,

84 pages,

and **5,362** words!

You finished the book! Your hard work paid off!

FUN AND GAMES!

THINK! Zelli is always available to help those in need. Think of a time when you helped someone who needed it.

FEEL! Bucket lied to Zelli about the goblins bullying her. How would it make you feel if someone took advantage of your kindness?

POOF.

ACT! It's okay to ask others for help. Make a list of friends and family who you could go to for help.

DIANE WALKER

(Madeleine Roux) is a *New York Times* bestselling author for children, young adults, and adults. A veteran Dungeons & Dragons player, Diane was raised in Minnesota, attended Beloit College in Wisconsin, and now lives with her two beloved blink dogs in Seattle, Washington.

TIM PROBERT is

the acclaimed illustrator of several middle grade books, including *Pickle*, the Rip & Red series, and the graphic novel series Lightfall for HarperAlley. Tim is an art director at the animation studio Nathan Love. He lives in New York with his wife and two cats.